What do you DO when a MONSTER says BOO?

by
Hope Vestergaard

pictures by
Maggie Smith

Dutton Children's Books

For Pilly, one of my favorite monsters,
and Janie, who said "*BOO!*"
—H.V.

To my big brother, Ben, who usually
knew what to do . . .
—M.S.

DUTTON CHILDREN'S BOOKS
A division of Penguin Young Readers Group

Published by the Penguin Group
Penguin Group (USA) Inc., 375 Hudson Street, New York, New York 10014, U.S.A.
Penguin Group (Canada), 90 Eglinton Avenue East, Suite 700, Toronto, Ontario, Canada
M4P 2Y3 (a division of Pearson Penguin Canada Inc.)
Penguin Books Ltd, 80 Strand, London WC2R 0RL, England
Penguin Ireland, 25 St Stephen's Green, Dublin 2, Ireland (a division of Penguin Books Ltd)
Penguin Group (Australia), 250 Camberwell Road, Camberwell, Victoria 3124, Australia
(a division of Pearson Australia Group Pty Ltd)
Penguin Books India Pvt Ltd, 11 Community Centre, Panchsheel Park, New Delhi - 110 017, India
Penguin Group (NZ), Cnr Airborne and Rosedale Roads, Albany, Auckland 1310, New Zealand
(a division of Pearson New Zealand Ltd)
Penguin Books (South Africa) (Pty) Ltd, 24 Sturdee Avenue, Rosebank, Johannesburg 2196, South Africa
Penguin Books Ltd, Registered Offices: 80 Strand, London WC2R 0RL, England

Text copyright © 2006 by Hope Vestergaard
Illustrations copyright © 2006 by Maggie Smith

Library of Congress Cataloging-in-Publication Data
Vestergaard, Hope.
      What do you do when a monster says boo? / by Hope Vestergaard; pictures by Maggie Smith.
         p.cm.
      Summary: Presents advice on how to deal with a monster.
      ISBN 0-525-47737-3
      [1. Monsters—Fiction. 2. Behavior—Fiction. 3. Stories in rhyme.] I. Smith, Maggie, ill. II. Title.
PZ8.3.V71266Wh 2005   [E]—dc21   2003049080

Published in the United States by Dutton Children's Books,
a division of Penguin Young Readers Group
345 Hudson Street, New York, New York 10014
www.penguin.com/youngreaders

Designed by Gloria Cheng & Abby Kuperstock

Manufactured in China
First Edition
10 9 8 7 6 5 4 3 2 1

What do you do when a monster says BOO?

Snatch up your blankets and bury your head?

Holler and howl and crawl under your bed?

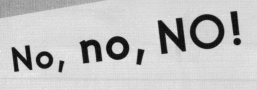

No, no, NO!
The best thing to do when
a monster says, "BOO!"
Is hold out your hand and say,
"How do you do?"

What do you do when a monster's breath stinks?

Cover your mouth and plug up your nose?

Put out the flames with a fire-truck hose?

No, no, NO!
The best thing to do when
a monster's breath stinks
Is find it a toothbrush and
show it the sink.

What do you do when a monster throws things?

Hide behind tables, the counter . . . a chair?

Lie low and act like you really don't care?

No, no, NO!

The best thing to do when
a monster throws things
Is give it a baseball and practice
your swings.

What do you do when a monster pulls hair?

Show it your teeth and pretend that you'll bite?

Forget all your manners and start a big fight?

No, no, NO!

The best thing to do when
a monster pulls hair
Is find its soft tummy and
tickle it there.

What do you do when a monster throws fits?

Hide in a closet and peek through the door?

Wait till it wearies and drops to the floor?

What do you do when a monster feels blue?

Ignore it completely and play with your games?

No, no, NO!

The best thing to do when
a monster feels blue
Is invite it on over to snuggle
with you.

What do you do when your monster just roars?

And roars . . .

And ROARS?

Do you grab a big pillow and give it a bop?

Cover your ears and demand that it stop?

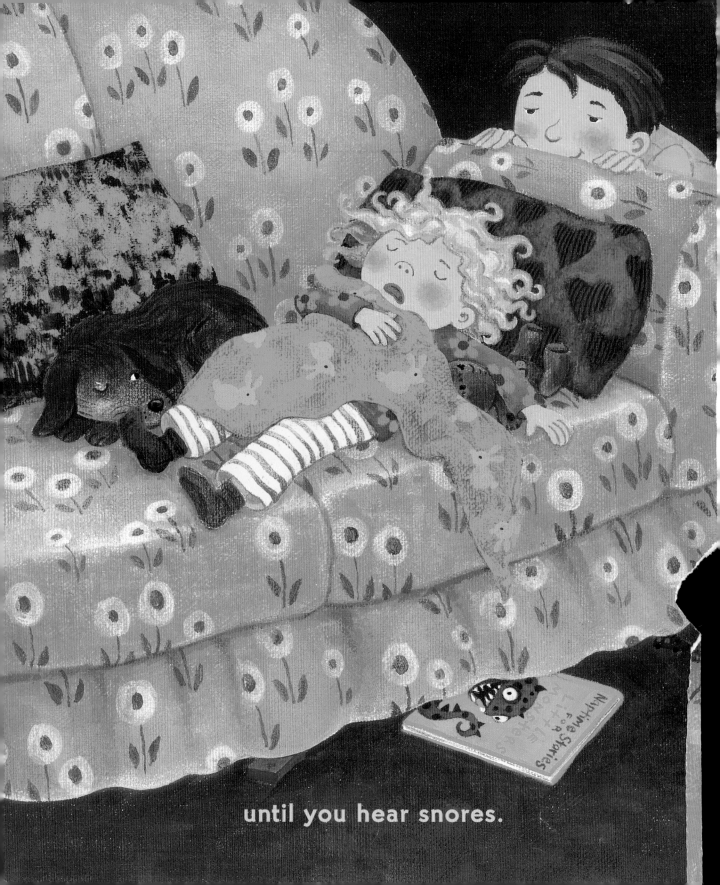

until you hear snores.